He swam down a little further into the deepening blue
and found the biggest creature he'd ever seen
singing a rumbly song.

"Excuse me," said Pipkin.
"How deep is the sea?"

"Deeper than a big blue whale like
ME has ever been," said the creature.
"Would you like to stay and sing to my
blue whale friends across the sea?"

"Sorry, I can't stop now," said Pipkin,
"I'm off to find the bottom of the sea."

The submarine took them down...

...and down...

...and down...

...to where the sea turned night-black
and there was no one else around.

Then, one by one,
twinkling lights began to appear.

All kinds of wonderful, lit-up creatures
were swimming around in the dark.

"Excuse me," said Pipkin.
"How deep is the sea?"

"Deep enough to have whole mountains at the bottom,"
said one of the twinkly creatures. "Look."

And sure enough, just below,
was a range of towering mountains...

"Is this the very deepest part?"
asked Pipkin.

Pipkin said to his Mama:

"The sea is very, VERY d
It's deep enough to hold
and deeper than a big blu
and deep enough to have
and lots of twinkly creat

"I wonder whether anyth
all the way down here?"

They peered into the d
but nothing came
So they sat for a whi
with miles a

"Ready

"Not quite," said the twinkly creature,
and it pointed to a valley. "Down there
is the very deepest part of the sea."

So the yellow submarin

It was very de

and very dark

and very,

very

quiet.

Flump went
as it landed o

The yellow submarine
them all the way back
to the top of the sea.

"And it's deep enough for very small penguins
to have very big adventures," said his Mama
as she rubbed him dry.

"I'm proud of you, my little Pip."

Come this way to see how deep Pipkin went.

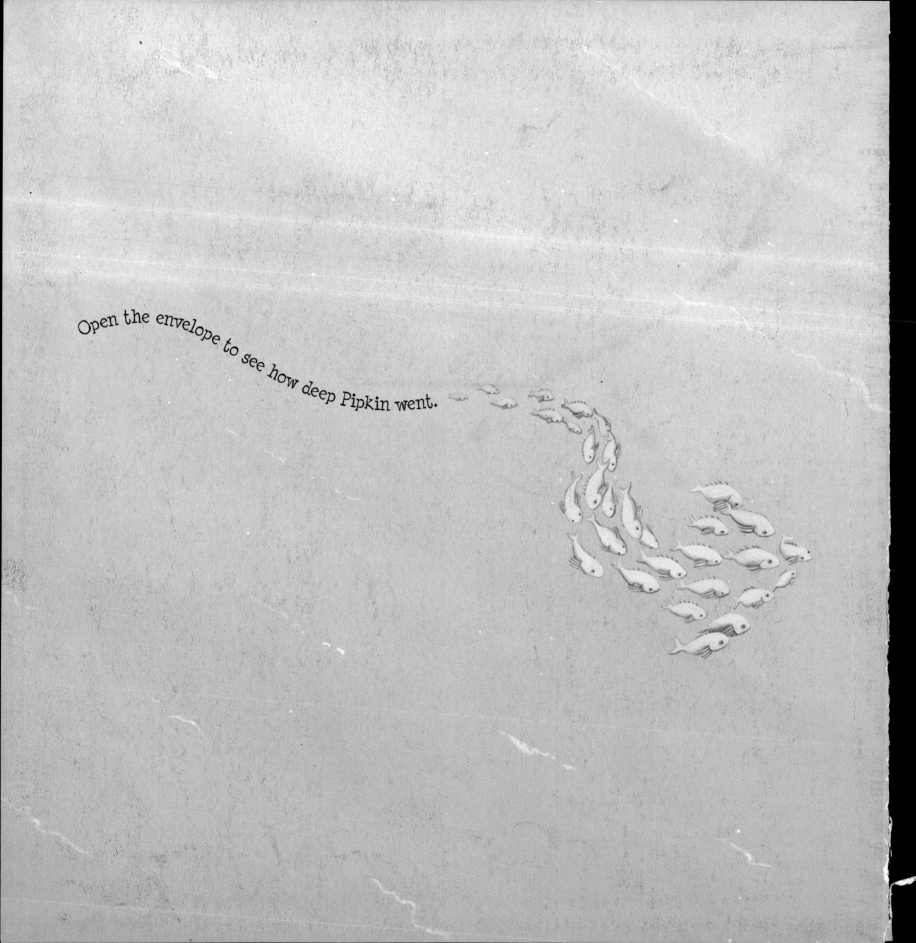

Open the envelope to see how deep Pipkin went.